Copyright © 1996 by Jon Buller and Susan Schade.
All rights reserved under International and Pan-American Copyright
Conventions. Published in the United States by Random House, Inc., New York,
and simultaneously in Canada by Random House of Canada Limited, Toronto.

http://www.randomhouse.com/

Library of Congress Cataloging-in-Publication Data
Schade, Susan.
Snow bugs / by Susan Schade and Jon Buller.
  p. cm. — (Bright & early book ; BE 29)
SUMMARY: The snow bugs discover wonderful ways to play on a snowy day.
ISBN 0-679-87913-7 (trade) — ISBN 0-679-97913-1 (lib. bdg.)
[1. Snow—Fiction. 2. Insects—Fiction. 3. Stories in rhyme.]
I. Buller, Jon, 1943–   . II. Title. III. Series.
PZ8.3. S287S1 1997
[E]—dc20
96-14239

Printed in the United States of America 10 9 8 7 6 5 4 3 2 1

GROLIER
BOOK CLUB EDITION

SNOW BUGS

by Susan Schade and Jon Buller

A Bright & Early Book

From BEGINNER BOOKS

A Division of Random House, Inc.

It's snowing.
It's blowing.

It's a snow day!

It's a play day!

Roll over and slide.

Throw snowballs and hide.

It's freezing!

They're sneezing.

Run back inside!

Bugs who are bare
need something to wear.

Find some wool.
Cut and pull.

Sit and knit.

Does it fit?

A sweater for Fran.
A sweater for Ann.

A blue scarf for Ed.
A green hat for Fred.

A snowsuit for Dot.
Four mittens for Spot.

Are we ready?
No, not yet.
This is what
we need to get...

a leather strip,
a paper clip,

a toothpick,
an ice cream stick,

a broken spoon,
a piece of string.

"Hop in, Dot,
that's everything!"

Oh, no!
TOO much snow!

What to do?
Shovel through!

Pulling and pushing.

Slipping . . .

and whooshing.

Sliding, gliding, riding.

WHEEEE!

Scoop and throw.

Ho, ho, ho!

Flap your wings.

Make snow things.

Then at night,
by candlelight...

a BUGS-ON-ICE SHOW!

Go, Dot, go!

Watch her score
a perfect ten.

"Hooray, Dot, skate again!"

Show bugs! Snow bugs!

Way to go, bugs!

BRIGHT and EARLY BOOKS
for BEGINNING Beginners